This ELMER book belongs to:

· ·

For Sabrina B. and Zoë Z.

This American edition published in 2012 for Books are Fun by Andersen Press Ltd.,
20 Vauxhall Bridge Road, London SW1V 2SA.
Text and Illustration copyright © David McKee, 1995
The rights of David McKee to be identified as the author and illustrator
of this work have been asserted by him in accordance with
the Copyright, Designs and Patents Act, 1988.
All rights reserved.
British Library Cataloguing in Publication Data available.

Color separated in Switzerland by Photolitho AG, Zürich.
Manufactured in China by C & C Offset Printing Co., Ltd.
1-C&C-6/26/12

ISBN 978 1 84939 546 5

ELMER
in the Snow

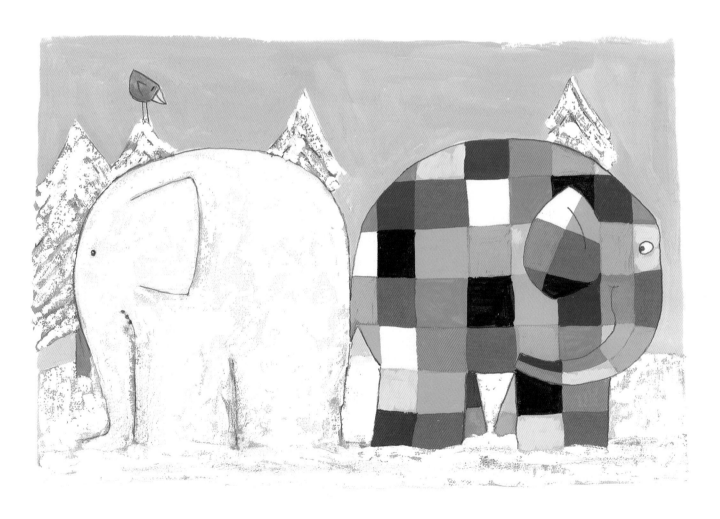

David McKee

Andersen Press

One morning, Elmer, the patchwork
elephant, met a group of elephants who
didn't look very happy.
"What's the matter?" asked Elmer.
"What's the matter is that it's cold," said one
of the elephants. "That's what's the matter."
"It's not really cold," said Elmer. "It's just a bit
colder than usual. What you need is a good walk to
warm you up. Come on, come with me."

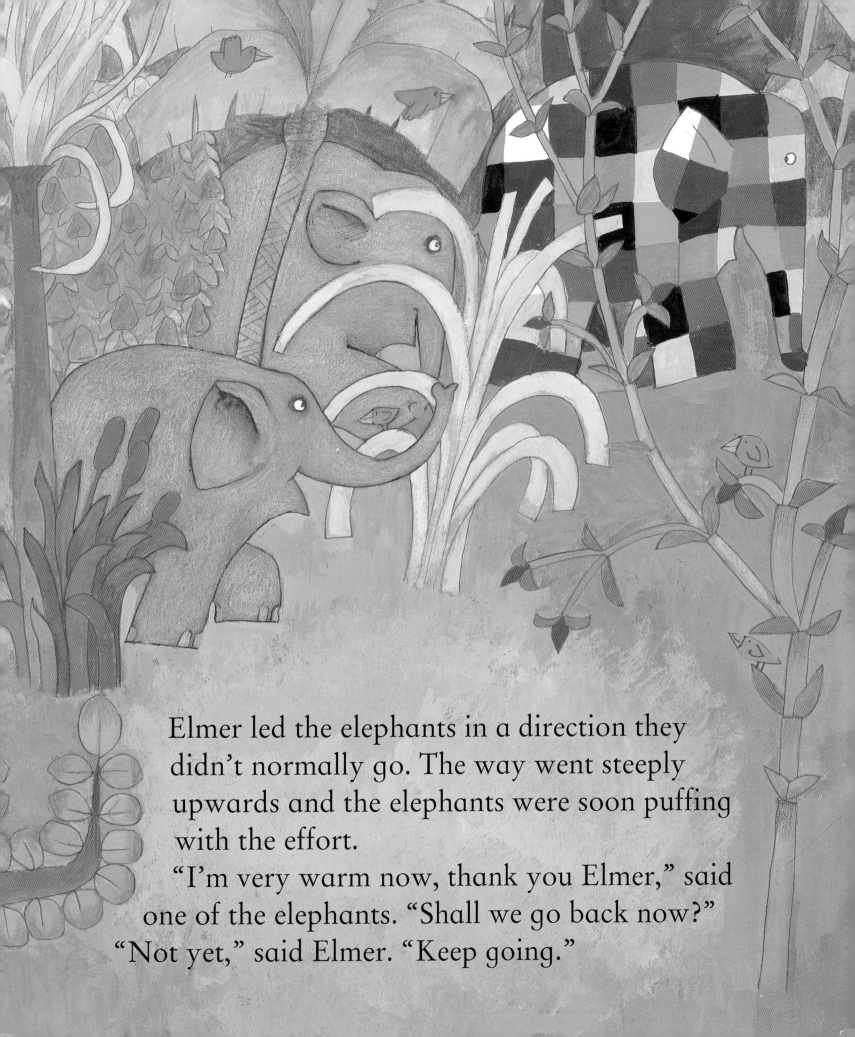

Elmer led the elephants in a direction they didn't normally go. The way went steeply upwards and the elephants were soon puffing with the effort.

"I'm very warm now, thank you Elmer," said one of the elephants. "Shall we go back now?"

"Not yet," said Elmer. "Keep going."

After they had gone further, an elephant said,
"Elmer, look at the trees, they're different here."
"That's because we are so high up," said Elmer.
"Come on, there's something I want to show you."

A little later the elephants came out into the open and they stared at the sight – everywhere was white. "SNOW!" they shouted. Although they had heard about snow, this was the first time they had actually seen any. The elephants rushed forward and roared with laughter as they played in the snow.

"It's really cold," called one of the elephants.

"Cold but fun," laughed another.

"Now, come and look at this," called Elmer. He was sliding on the ice of a pond that had frozen solid. One by one the others curiously joined him.

Soon the elephants were slipping and sliding and crashing and falling and really enjoying themselves. They didn't notice Elmer quietly sneak away.

The elephants forgot all about Elmer until they heard his voice nearby.
"Help! Help! I've frozen solid."
The elephants stopped playing and hurried to find Elmer. To their dismay, there stood a white elephant.
"He has, he's frozen solid," gasped one of the elephants.

Then he touched the white elephant and a
piece fell off. "It's made of snow," he said.
"I know where Elmer is," chuckled another. He pointed
to a line of footprints in the snow.
"Come on."

The elephants followed the line of footprints but before
they reached him, Elmer appeared and with a laugh,
started throwing snowballs that he had already prepared.

It wasn't long before all the elephants were throwing snowballs at each other.

"It's starting to snow quite hard," said Elmer after a while. "It's time for us to go." Still laughing and playing, and with the snow falling all around them, the elephants hurried back to the trees and then on home.

When they were finally home again,
one of the elephants said, "Snow is fun,
but it really is cold."
"Yes," said another. "It's nice to be back where it's warm."
Elmer said nothing. He just smiled.

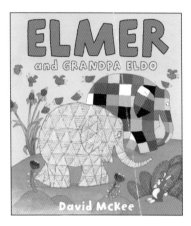

ELMER and GRANDPA ELDO

David McKee

David McKee

ELMER AGAIN

ELMER in the Snow

David McKee

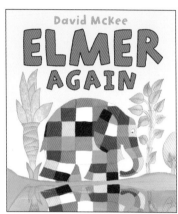

ELMER and WILBUR

David McKee

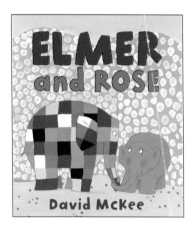

ELMER and ROSE

David McKee

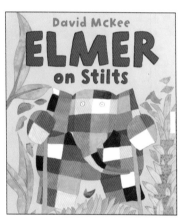

David McKee

ELMER on Stilts

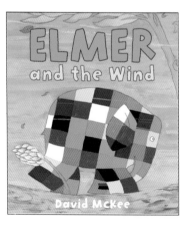

ELMER and the Wind

David McKee

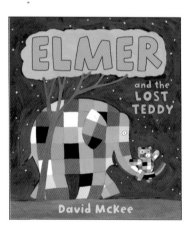

ELMER and the LOST TEDDY

David McKee

Enjoy more Elmer stories from:

www.andersenpressusa.com

www.lernerbooks.com

www.oceanhousemedia.com